Jan Kjær & Merlin P. Mann

TAYNIKMA

Book 1: Master Thief

Para mis suegros, Bertha y Bolívar,
y mi cuñada Veronica, por enseñarme
su maravilloso país, Ecuador.
Jan Kjær

For William.
Merlin P. Mann

Young World Digital
MMVIII

TAYNIKMA
Book 1: Master Thief
(Original title: Mestertyven)

Translated by Merlin P. Mann

ISBN 978-0-9558337-0-0
First edition

Published by:
Young World Digital Ltd • PO Box 6268 • London W1A 2HE
www.youngworlddigital.com

Printed and bound in Great Britain in 2008
by Stanley L. Hunt (Printers) Ltd, Rushden, Northants

British Library Cataloguing in Publication Data available.

TAYNIKMA
Book 1: Master Thief
Book 2: The Rats
Book 3: Tower of the Sun
Book 4: The Lost Catacombs
Book 5: The Secret Arena
Book 6: Duel of the Clans
Book 7: Henzel's Ambush
Book 8: The Forest of Shadows
Book 9: The Fortress of Light
Book 10: The Final Battle

www.taynikma.co.uk

TAYNIKMA

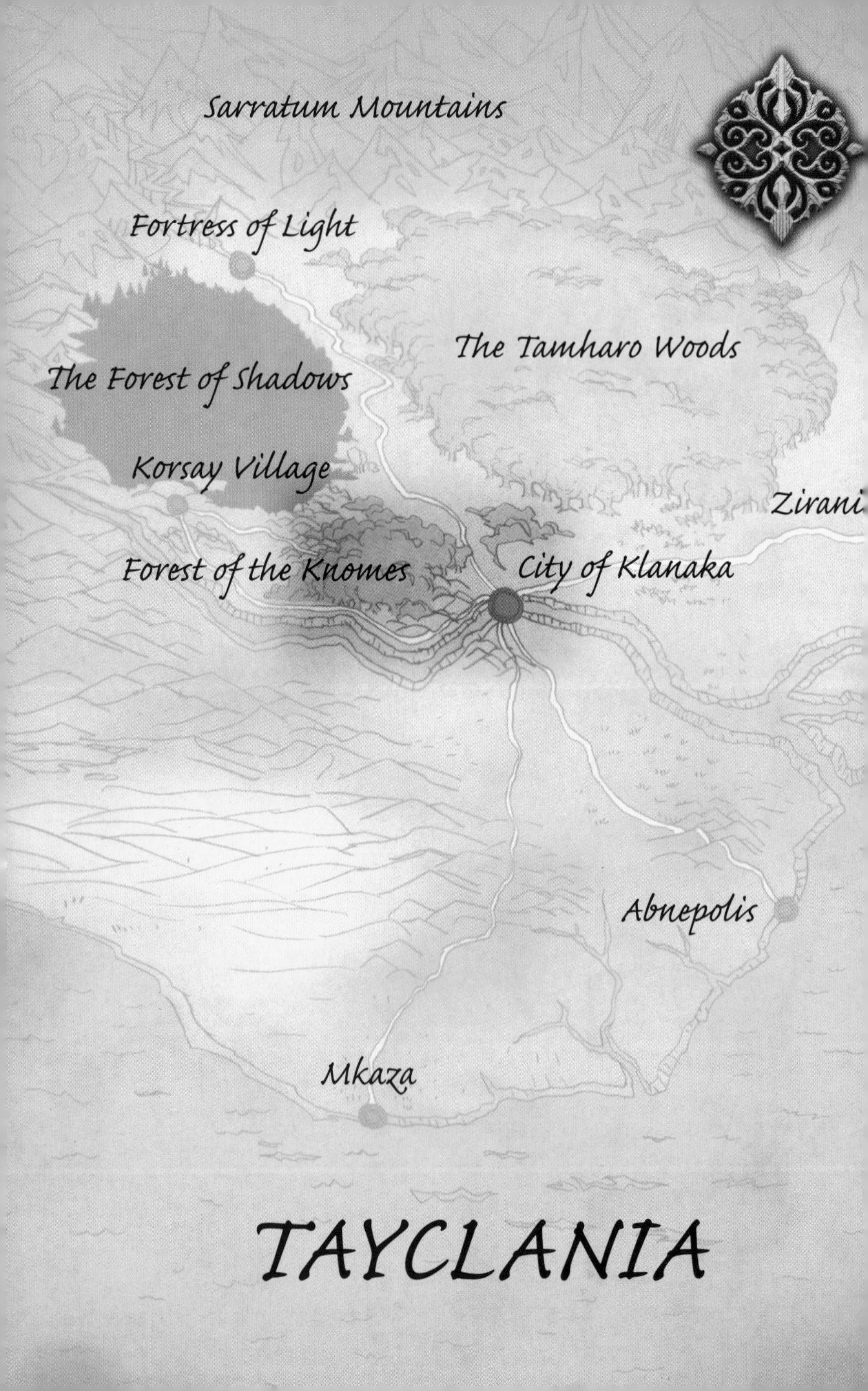

Sarratum Mountains

Fortress of Light

The Tamharo Woods

The Forest of Shadows

Korsay Village

Zirani

Forest of the Knomes

City of Klanaka

Abnepolis

Mkaza

TAYCLANIA

The Land of Tayclania

South of the mountains, north of the sea lies Tayclania.

For hundreds of years it was a haven for merchants, craftsmen and scholars. A land ruled by four clans: The Sun, The Moon, The Mountain and The River Clans.

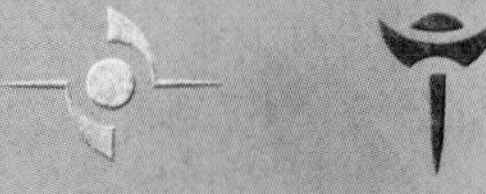 

Each clan had its own deities and powers. The Sun Clan had the healing powers of light, the Moon Clan had the protection of shadow, the Mountain Clan had raw strength, and the River Clan had wisdom.

Even though it was a land of plenty, quarrels began to break out between the clans. The quarrels lead to fights. The fights lead to war.

A treaty was signed, but few believed the four clans could rule together again.

Peace was short-lived. A sorceress murdered three champions from each clan and from their souls she created 12 invincible knights: the Sentinels. Soon all of Tayclania had to bow to her rule and she became The Empress.

The clans were outlawed, the borders were closed and The Empress imposed the Law of the Sun. She declared that only by having just one deity could the land live in peace and harmony. A brief uprising was attempted by the clans but was easily crushed by the Sentinels.

Soon the rule of the immortal Empress of Light will have lasted for 100 years.

Koto

14-year-old Koto grew up with his mum and dad in the small village of Korsay by the foot of the Sarratum Mountains.

They are very poor and one day Koto had to travel to the large city of Klanaka to raise money for the family.

Koto is a brave kid with a heart for adventure. He is very agile and is particularly skilled at hiding in shadows. He also has the ability of night vision – an ability he didn't inherit from his mum and dad.

WELCOME TO TAYNIKMA!

You are about to embark on a fantastic journey with Koto and his friends. The story takes place in a world quite different from ours where you'll stumble upon fascinating places and creatures.

Taynikma is no ordinary book, nor is it an ordinary comic book. It's a special mix of adventure, action and magic. Each book also holds four pages of tips and tricks for drawing the Taynikma-style.

The story of Koto spans 10 books, so make sure your collection is complete.

Visit our website: www.taynikma.co.uk for the latest news about the series.

Have a great journey!

Jan Kjær & Merlin P. Mann

Book 1: Master Thief

Forest of the Knomes

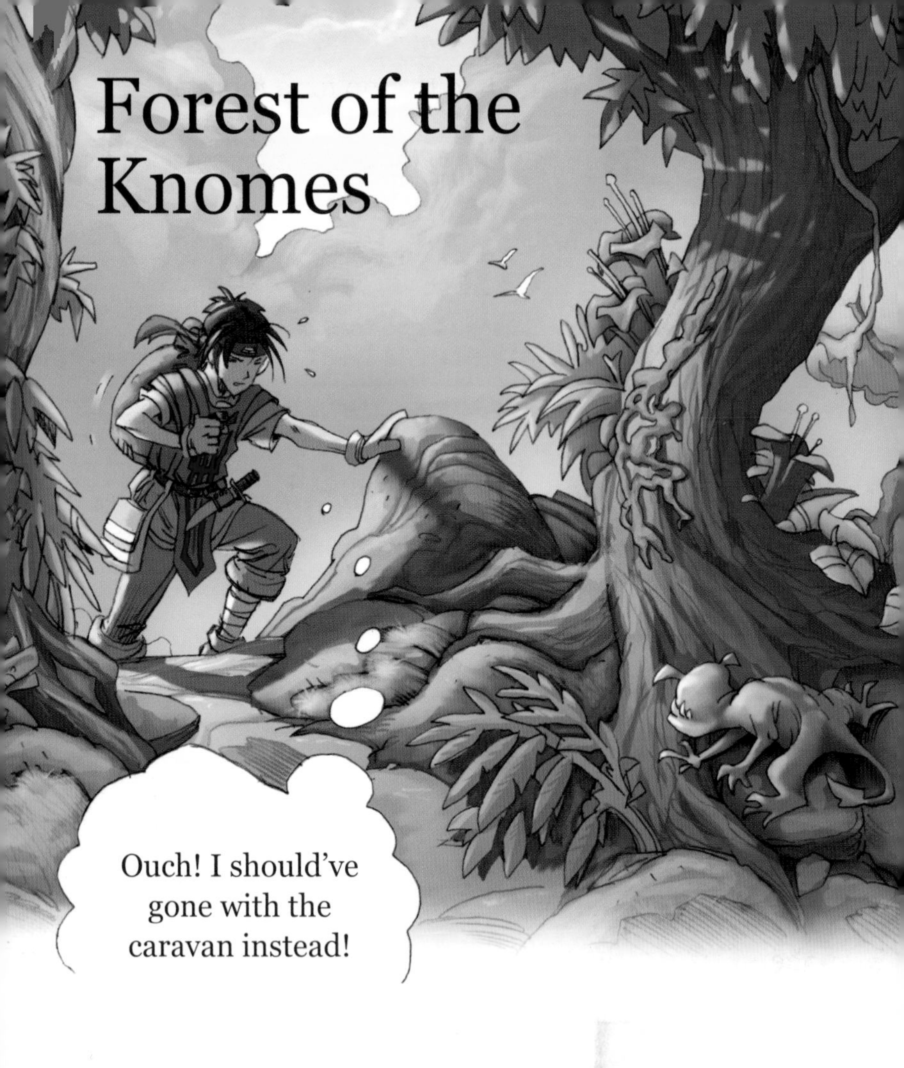

»But three silver coins for a trip to Klanaka! That's more than mum and dad can spare ...«

Koto was travelling through the Forest of the Knomes. He knew it was dangerous, but he was in a hurry. On foot this was the fastest route to the city of Klanaka.

Koto was exhausted and had to stop for a moment.

Not that this made him much calmer. Who had hung a mask right there? Koto knew many a story about the wild, thieving Knomes, but never met anyone who'd actually seen them. Hopefully they were just old wives' tales ...

Koto hid behind the tree and pulled a small package from his sack. »They won't get this from me,« he thought and hid the package under his shirt.

The sack landed on the ground and the Knomes jumped it like a pack of mad dogs.

»I hope that keeps them occupied,« thought Koto and hurried across the glade to the thick forest on the other side.

But it was not enough for the Knomes. Koto had only taken a few steps before one of them started yelling and pointing towards him. Time to run!

The razor-sharp leaf barely missed Koto, as he skipped through the bushes. The Knomes were right on his tail. Koto's heart beat like never before. Being the best at hide-and-seek was fine for playing with friends back home – but the Knomes didn't look too playful. This was for real.

Koto noticed a large tree just as the Knomes rushed through the shrubs. He leapt into the tree's shadow – and it was as if the darkness put a veil over him! Koto jumped high up in the air and got hold of two sturdy branches. He held on with all his strength and suddenly he seemed to blend into the shadow.

Two of the Knomes went on, but the largest one stayed behind – right below the tree! Koto held his breath as well as he could, but a large drop of sweat was slowly trickling down his forehead. Now what? If he let go with one hand, he would surely fall. Koto closed his eyes and hoped for the best.

»Ni--?« said the Knome and looked up at Koto!

The Knome was knocked out by the fall. Koto got on his feet and saw the two other Knomes rushing towards him.

Just as he was about to run, he noticed that part of the shadow had stuck to his shirt like a thick cobweb. »What's this?« thought Koto as he pulled off the strange shadow strings. Then he had an idea!

Koto had to get away, while the little pests were still on the ground. He ran as fast as he could – and didn't notice the mysterious figure standing among the trees not far away.

Before Koto knew what hit him, the enchanted vines had trapped his arms and legs.

»Only a fool would think he could travel through my forest without permission!« said a mysterious voice from between the trees. A tall figure moved gracefully towards him. The angry Knomes were already on their feet again, and Koto tried desperately to escape, but the vines were way too strong a trap.

»Don't touch it,« yelled Koto, but the girl took no notice of his demands.

»A present for Princess Zika, perhaps?« said the girl with a smirk as she picked up the package.

»It's an heirloom!« said Koto. »If I lose it, my mum and dad will lose everything.«

The girl looked curiously at Koto. He felt a strange sensation inside. As if she could see his very thoughts. She untied the string around the package and opened it carefully.

»Tay-what ...?« asked Koto and gave the girl a confused look.

»Where did you get this?« she asked and looked at Koto quite differently from before.

»My mum and dad gave it to me,« said Koto. »I don't have a clue what it is, but I have to take it to the city to sell it. Or else we won't have enough money to pay Lord Tuskan – and we'll lose our home – and –«

»Easy now!« said the girl. »You'll have to tell the story from the beginning.«

Koto took a deep breath, and then he began:

»I come from the village Korsay. We live at the brick maker's, where my mum and dad have worked all their lives. We make bricks for the city of Klanaka, but a few days ago something happened ...«

»My mum and dad walked out into the yard to talk to Brick Master Kayton.«

»My dad couldn't believe what he was hearing. "But the house has been ours for years," he said. Kayton simply replied: "That's come to an end now! We need to make more bricks for the huge castle up at the pass. Orders of the Empress. There's nothing I can do."

My mum couldn't hold back her tears any longer.«

»Kayton didn't like to see my mum cry. I guess he hoped to comfort her by saying: "Easy, Gyrt! I talked to Lord Tuskan, and he has another small house you can buy."

"Buy?" asked my dad. "How much will that be?"

"300 coins," said Kayton. And he even smiled.«

WHAT?!

It will take us years to make that much money!

»I'm sure you have something you can sell. The slaves won't arrive for another couple of months. You'll have plenty of time to get the money together."

We were all very sad that evening.«

»I had no idea what my dad was talking about, but then he put a strange object on the table. It was wrapped in an old cloth. My dad was just about to tell me something, when my mum interrupted. "It's just an old heirloom," she said.«

Koto shook his head.

»I don't think you even know who you are,« she whispered. For a moment she just stood there thinking. Then she waved her hand and said: »Dendra! Zimito!«

Koto landed flat on his stomach as the vines suddenly let go of him.

»I don't know what fate has in store for you,« said Princess Zika. »But you need to take good care. There are many things you don't know yet!«

What was that supposed to mean? Koto didn't have a clue, but he got his heirloom and the slightly damaged sack back. The princess gave him a worried look and had the Knomes escort him out of the forest.

Was the hardest part of the journey over now? Or was this only the beginning?

Klanaka

»Holy goat!« gasped Koto as he saw the gigantic city wall. And the town on the other side was even grander.

Waves of people pushed in and out of the huge gates. Koto hesitated for a while, but soon he was dragged into Klanaka by the crowds.

Many hagglers and tradesmen sat by the walls selling and bargaining. Koto watched them for a while, as he thought about Zika's words: take good care.

Koto spotted a couple of soldiers. Asking the city guards had to be safer than dealing with sneaky looking merchants. They could cheat you.

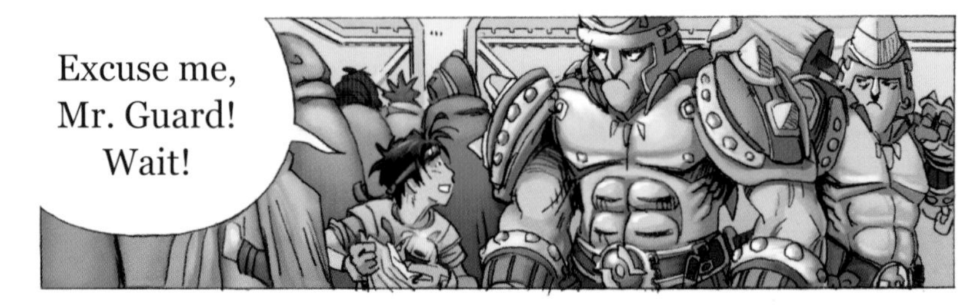

Koto held out the heirloom and asked: »Do you know where I could sell something like this?«

The soldier was just about to push him aside, when a voice from a horseman behind him called out: »Wait! Let me see!« The rider was obviously the leader of the soldiers. He approached Koto.

»Where did you steal that, you rascal?« he said spitefully, looking at Koto like he was nothing more than a filthy animal.

»Don’t you know who I am?« hissed the rider.

I am
Captain Henzel!

Head of the city
guards and the
mighty protector
of Klanaka!

Koto took a step backwards. This was not going as he had planned.

»Why, catch him, you fools!« shrieked Captain Henzel to the two big soldiers.

»Over here! QUICK!« a voice suddenly cried out. Koto looked around. Where did that come from? There! A narrow crack in the wall.

»Idiots! The brat has a nikma!« yelled Captain Henzel. »Catch him! NOW!«

»Hey! We gotta move fast!« said the voice. Koto could finally see who was speaking in the dark – a skinny guy with a long tail!

Koto hesitated, but when he saw the soldiers climbing over the wall he knew he had no choice. »Better this, than being caught by a pack of brutes ...« he thought.

»AAH!« cried Koto. There was no floor underneath the grating. Just a slippery, muddy slope leading straight into the dark below ...

Koto landed right in a canal of disgusting water. »Phew! What a stench!« he gasped and tried all he could to keep his face above water.

»Up here,« said Sneak and jumped up on a ladder. Koto had no idea if Sneak could be trusted, but there was no other way out. He followed the skinny guy up the ladder.

Sneak opened a trapdoor and crawled up into a dark warehouse filled with tall stacks of boxes and crates.

Koto jumped as he noticed a large, burly figure by the crates, but Sneak merely smiled.

»Take it easy. He's my trusted companion,« said Sneak and waved at the boy. »Bully! Come over and say hello to our new friend!«

»He doesn't look so fierce up close,« thought Koto.

»What made you show your nikma to Captain Henzel and the city guards?«

»What's a nikma?« asked Koto. The thin smile on Sneak's face got even wider.

»I bet you just arrived here, right?« said Sneak and winked at Bully. »Luckily you now have a couple of mates like me and Bully here!«

Sneak walked over to Koto and pointed at the thing in his sack. »THAT is a nikma,« said Sneak. »They've been illegal for ages, but I know people who buy them. Can I see it?«

Koto was very unsure, but after all that was exactly why he was here. To sell the thing. Carefully he placed the nikma on top of some boxes.

»But nothing's impossible!« Sneak walked over to a rack of weird tools. »I've got something to show you, boy,« he said and waved at Koto to make him come closer. Koto didn't move. He looked at Bully, who simply smiled back at him with a friendly face.

Koto took a step towards Sneak, who had grabbed a strange metal ball. It was linked to a heavy beam with a sturdy chain.

»Aww! Such a shame!« laughed Sneak. »Welcome to the big city, farm boy!«

Koto pulled as hard as he could, but he was trapped!

»Get the nikma, Bully!« said Sneak. »Bye-bye!«

Koto had to do something quick. He couldn't pull off the chain, but he had to stop the thieves.

Just then he noticed a strong shadow from a pile of boxes and he remembered the incident in the forest. Koto had ripped off part of the shadow.

Could he do it again?

»What the–?« was all Sneak managed to say before the tall stack of boxes crashed right down on top of him!

The boxes knocked Sneak unconscious, but Bully had gotten away! Koto noticed how the gate to the street outside had been knocked open.

A long time went by, before someone finally looked in through the open gate ...

»Over here, Sir!« yelled a soldier. Unfortunately it was one of Henzel's guards who had heard Koto's cries. And Koto was still stuck in the trap.

Captain Henzel walked over to Koto. He had the guards break the chain and tie Koto's hands behind his back.

»Where is the nikma?« asked Henzel and grabbed Koto's chin. Koto hesitated, but Henzel was not going to wait long for an answer ...

Captain Henzel kicked a stack of crates, and the grimace on his face suggested a pain in his foot.

»Take the thief and his buddy to the prison cells,« gnarled Henzel, as the guards pulled the unconscious Sneak from the boxes in order to tie him up.

»When I return from my council with the Sentinels, I will get the truth from the little miscreants myself,« continued Henzel and rushed from the warehouse. Koto was dragged outside and thrown onto a wagon.

The soldiers went back in to fetch Sneak, when Koto noticed a man standing by the warehouse. His face was covered by a cloak with strange ornaments, but Koto still felt his piercing gaze. He had obviously watched the whole scene. Who was this man?

The Prison Cells

»I'm sorry I can't fit you in a proper cell,« cackled the prison guard.

Koto and Sneak had been thrown in each a dog cage. It was impossible to stand and if they wanted to lie down, their legs would stick out through the bars.

Koto was not at all keen on spending the night in a cage like this.

»Don't worry! We'll soon have an empty cell for you,« said the guard as he left the hallway. »We're selling lots of slaves at the time – hee hee hee!«

Koto said nothing. He was busy trying to find a way of sitting that wasn't painful.

»Captain Henzel will fry you, silly boy,« laughed Sneak.

»What do you mean?« asked Koto. »You'll be questioned too, won't you?«

»As soon as The Rats learn that I've been caught, they'll send someone to buy my way out!« said Sneak.

»The Rats?« asked Koto.

»That's my gang! The toughest pickpockets in Klanaka!« answered Sneak proudly.

»You can't buy someone out of prison!« said Koto.

»Fool! Hundreds of people are thrown in jail,« said Sneak. »Who do you think will notice if some are sold off as slaves?«

Koto shook his head. Was it impossible to find an honest person in this city?

The guard was about to lead the man further on, but the cloak-clad visitor stopped in front of the dog pens. Koto couldn't see his face, but there was something familiar about him.

The ornaments!

Koto recognized the cloak – this had to be the man from outside the warehouse.

»That's the one I'm looking for,« said the man and pointed straight at Koto.

The guard was about to object, but as the man handed him a small leather pouch, he merely smiled. The guard grabbed the pouch and unlocked Koto's cage door.

»Wait!« cried Sneak. »You're making a mistake!«

Koto crawled out of the cage and looked at the tall man. »Who are you?« asked Koto, but the man didn't respond at all. He just started walking towards the door and Koto hurried after him. There was no reason to sit here and wait for Captain Henzel to return ...

Master Gekko

The man walked in silence all the way to the old tower at the far end of town. He gave Koto a small push up the stairs to a large attic filled with books and strange pots. Apparently this was where the man lived.

»I am Master Gekko,« he finally uttered.

»My name is Koto – from Korsay,« replied Koto, but Gekko did not respond. He merely walked to the old crooked window to pull in a barrel of rain water. He poured the water into a kettle.

»Dragon or Apple?« asked Master Gekko.

»Tea!« continued Gekko impatiently. »Do you want Dragon-tea or Apple-tea?«

»Oh … I …« said Koto. Gekko sighed and poured some leaves from a tin into the kettle.

»The chest by the window,« said Gekko and pointed.

»Mr. Gekko,« said Koto politely. »I guess you bought me to be your slave, but I have an important duty.«

»MASTER Gekko!« he growled.

»I'm sorry … Master Gekko,« said Koto. »B-but, I have to collect 300 coins. Or else we'll lose the house, and …«

»Go to the chest!« interrupted Master Gekko. »Tunga is waiting!« Who? Koto was just about to ask, but the look on Gekko's face made him keep quiet.

The chest gave a clicking sound, when Koto lifted the lid. It was empty. Koto gave a confused look.

»Here comes Tunga. He keeps away burglars,« said Gekko with a hint of a smile.

There was only one way out – the window!

Koto barely got hold of the shadow below the sill.

»But now what? Is he trying to kill me, or what?« thought Koto.

Master Gekko grabbed Koto by the neck and pulled him back inside. »I knew it,« he said, and he almost looked excited. »Your shadow powers have been woken.«

»My what?« gasped Koto.

»You cannot control them yet,« said Master Gekko and returned to the fireplace. »So far only your fear or anger will trigger the powers. But with my help you can master your abilities.«

»I'm not here to master anything,« said Koto and got up quickly.

»I ... I was going to sell that nikma ... and bring back the money ...« answered Koto.

»Listen, young lad!« said Master Gekko in a hard voice. »I can help you get back the nikma, but there is something you need to do for me first!«

»When you are able to master your powers ...« said Master Gekko.

The Castle

»The opening is too small for me,« whispered Gekko. »But you should be able to squeeze through it.«

Koto looked at the pitch black moat water and wasn't really eager for a swim.

Gekko had explained the route several times. Koto was to swim through the sewer, up to a warehouse and cross the yard to Henzel's tower.

»You know what to look for, right?« asked Gekko and gave Koto a very serious glance.

»Sure! Some scrolls. With a Sun insignia.«

»And no snooping around,« said Gekko. »Quick in and quick out – that's how a thief stays alive.«

Both Gekko and Koto held their breath, when the hook slammed into the wall on the other side. Hopefully the guards up on the wall hadn't heard the sound.

Koto slid slowly into the water. It was cold! He grabbed hold of the rope and pulled himself over. He was about to become a thief. Not exactly what his mum had in mind, but what was he supposed to do? It was the only way he could help them. He looked back at Gekko, who was still hiding in the bushes.

Koto dived into the dark water along the castle wall.

Koto swallowed a lot of the dark water before he surfaced on the other side. He tried all he could not to cough too loudly.

Koto looked anxiously around the warehouse. He had always had excellent eyesight at night, but it seemed like his vision was better than ever now. Maybe this had something to do with the shadow powers as well?

He sneaked quietly over to the door and opened it just enough to squeeze through. The skies were clear and the light from the moon had the towers cast long shadows over the yard.

Koto stepped carefully out into the yard. He made sure he stayed in the shadows. They were his only hiding place.

»Hello!« A hoarse voice called out and Koto's heart almost stopped. »Hello, Boffo! The door to the warehouse is open!«

Koto looked back. He hadn't closed the door, and now he could see two guards walking toward the warehouse. He stood perfectly still in the shadow.

The guards walked over to the door and looked inside. Koto moved on very carefully – but he didn't make it all the way to the tower before the guards turned around and looked out into the yard.

»I hope the shadow is enough cover ...« thought Koto.

»Come on Boffo! Our beers are gettin' warm!« said the guard and dragged the other guard with him.

»Phew,« thought Koto. »That was close!«

He got to Henzel's tower and looked up at the tall building. It would be a far climb to the top window, but this was where Koto had to enter.

Koto tied the climbing claws to his hands and feet and began scaling the tower wall like a spider. He was very careful not to look down. If he lost his grip, he would be done for.

»You have to be a dwarf burglar to get in here,« thought Koto and wiped the sweat from his forehead. He was in a room filled with clothes. »There's enough here for an entire village,« thought Koto. But it all belonged to Henzel. Koto sneaked to the door.

»There!« thought Koto and stepped over to the table. The two scrolls were both sealed with a Sun insignia. Koto quickly stuck them in his sack – when suddenly he eyed something in the moonlight.

»That necklace must be worth hundreds of coins,« thought Koto. »Mum and dad could give that to Lord Tuskan!«

Koto grabbed the necklace, but it was stuck. He pulled it a couple of times before he noticed a bell ringing in another room. »What's that?« thought Koto, but as the door was opened he finally realized it. He had triggered an alarm!

»Who's there?« hollered a voice. Captain Henzel was standing by the door in his night shirt and a silly-looking hat. He carried a lamp in one hand and a rapier in the other.

»You again?! Get over here, you brat!« screamed Henzel and lunged at Koto.

»Get down from there, culprit!« hissed Henzel as he tried to get the night hat out of his eyes. Koto reached desperately for the shadow behind him – and got hold of it. He tore off a thick string and managed to make it stick to a wooden beam under the roof. Now he could use it as a rope.

Henzel fell backwards, while Koto landed on his feet like a cat.

»No time for long goodbyes ...« thought Koto and rushed out the door.

Koto ran down the stairs to the main door. Out in the yard he could see the guards thundering towards him. Koto sprinted as fast as he could over to the warehouse and jumped inside.

Koto swam through the grate and back into the moat.

»Arm your crossbows!« screamed a guard from up on the castle wall.

Koto gasped. He would be far too easy a target down here in the water.

»Stay below the shadow,« whispered Master Gekko from the other side of the moat – and then Koto noticed how a shadow was floating in the air above him. Was this Master Gekko's doing?

The guards fired aimlessly into the water, but Koto was already safe on the other side.

Gekko was in a great mood once they got back home. »You did well, lad!« he said. But Koto was far from happy.

If I had gotten the necklace with me, I could have bought that house for mum and dad. I'm no proper thief!

»You will be,« said Gekko sternly. »I want you to be my apprentice. I can make you the greatest thief ever. You will easily be able to provide for your parents then!«

»Are you sure?« asked Koto. Master Gekko smiled and put his hand on Koto's shoulder.

»You don't know the powers you hold,« said Gekko. »Your adventure has just begun ...«

Follow the adventures of Koto in Book 2: **The Rats**

Win a Book!

Here's your chance to get a free copy of a Taynikma-book.

FAN ART

Draw your own version of one of the cool scenes from Taynikma. Try your hand at illustrating Koto and the Knomes, or one of your own ideas?

Send us your drawings, and if we like them, we'll publish them in one of the future Taynikma-books – and you will get the book for free!

LETTERS FROM THE READERS

We would also love to hear all your comments and questions about Taynikma. Ever wondered why Koto's eyes turn red when in the dark? Or what Gekko's favourite tea is?

SEND YOUR FAN ART AND LETTERS TO:

Taynikma
PO Box 6268
London W1A 2HE

Or by e-mail to: mail@taynikma.co.uk

Art School

Koto's Head

If you want to draw Koto's head, you'll need some guidelines. Here's what to do:

1. Draw an oblong circle and spilt it down the middle, both horizontally and vertically.

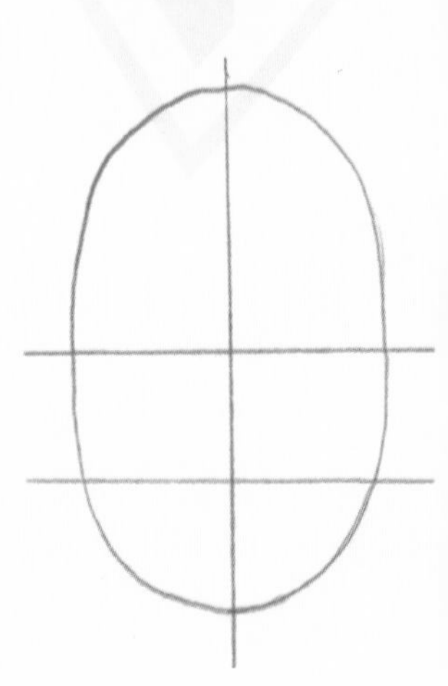

In the lower half, draw another vertical line in the middle.

These are your guidelines.

2. Now you can draw the face.

The eyes should be right below the centre-line.

The nose is a bit to the right of the vertical line and touches the bottom horizontal line.

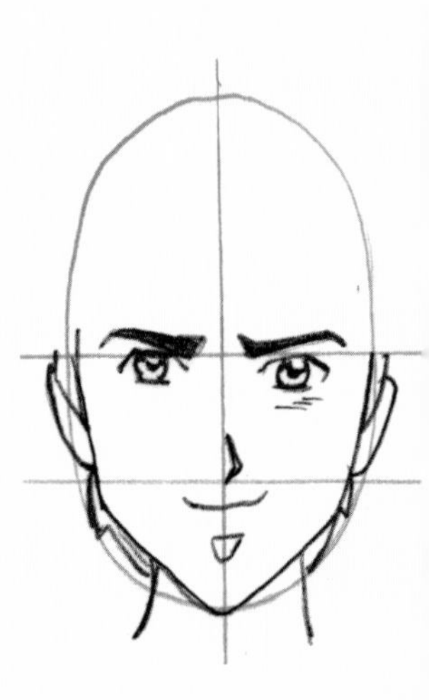

Now it's time for the mouth – remember the sharp jaw and the pointy chin. Those are some of Koto's recognizable features.

3. Place a dot right in the forehead.

From this dot you can draw the hair that lies on Koto's forehead.

4. Between this hair and the eyes, draw the headband.

And behind the hair on the forehead, draw a second set of spiky-looking hair for the rest of the head.

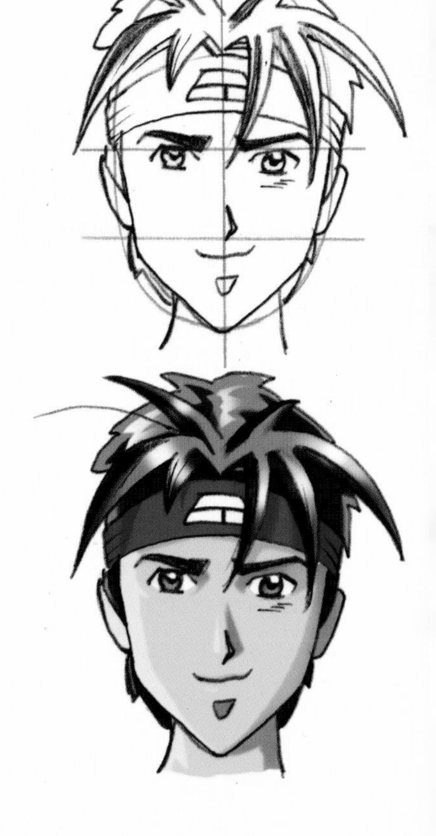

5. Now it's time for colouring.

Taynikma is coloured on the computer. You'll learn more about that later on.

Bend your joints

Don't worry. It's not gymnastics, but dynamic drawing.

A beginner will typically draw their figures with stiff joints – that means straight arms, legs, fingers and so on. That's not the natural way and it looks terrible:

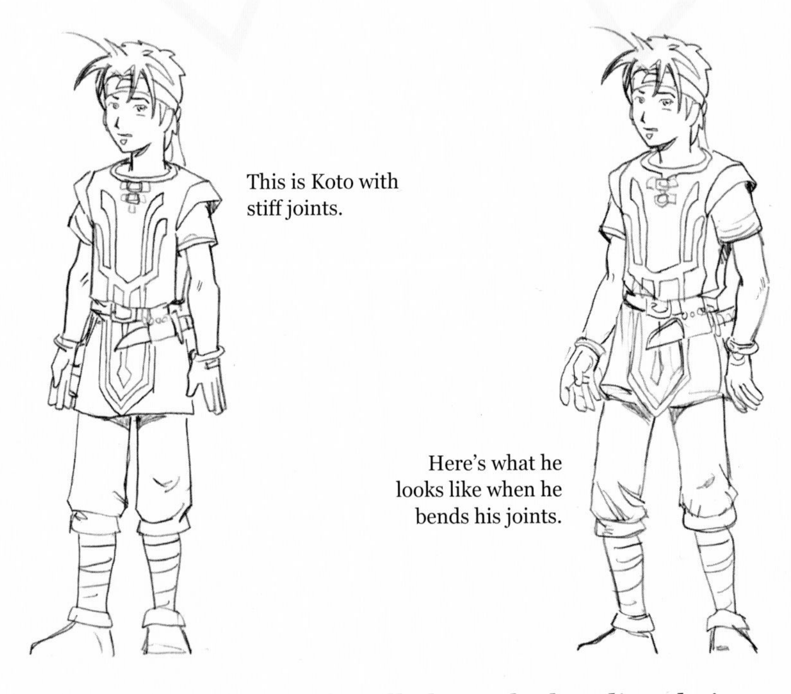

This is Koto with stiff joints.

Here's what he looks like when he bends his joints.

Both people and animals will always be bending their joints a bit. It doesn't matter if we're moving or standing still. We'll always have a slight bend in the elbows, wrists, knees etc.

So why do you need to know that? Well, if you soften the joints, you will have a far more natural looking drawing.

This also goes for imaginary creatures.

This is an ‘***eek***’, one of Koto’s adversaries in book 2: **The Rats.**

This is how many joints an eek has.

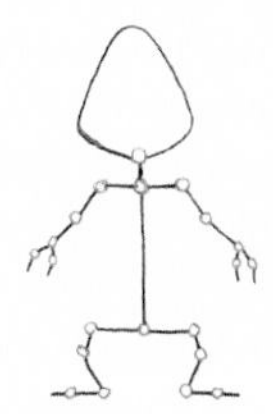

I could draw it with stiff joints since that would be easier.

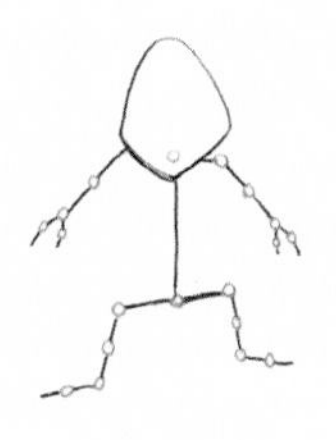

But if I really want my drawing to look alive, I need to put in a bit more effort and try to get it to bend in every joint. Don’t you agree that looks better?

TAYNIKMA is a series of ten books!

Follow the adventures of Koto in book 2:
"The Rats"

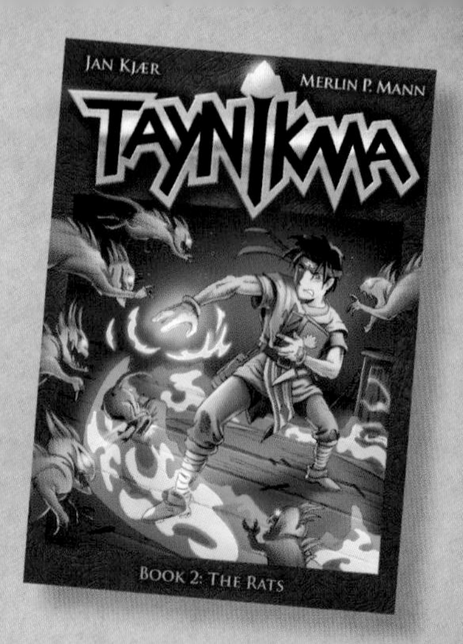

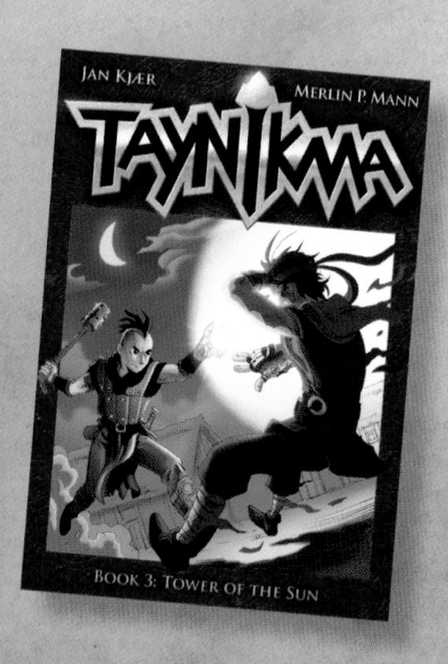

Book 3 and 4 will appear in August 2008
- ask at your local book dealer

Check for news and updates on our website
www.taynikma.co.uk